The Smallest Pirate

By the same authors

The Smallest Pirate

Story and Pictures by

Denise and Alain Trez

THE VIKING PRESS   NEW YORK

First Edition

Translated by Douglas McKee
Copyright © 1970 by Denise and Alain Trez
All rights reserved

First published in 1970 by The Viking Press, Inc.
625 Madison Avenue, New York, N.Y. 10022

Published simultaneously in Canada by
The Macmillan Company of Canada Limited
Trade 670—65223—7   VLB 670—65224—5
Library of Congress catalog card number: 75—123015
Printed in U.S.A.

Pic Bk

1   2   3   4   5   74   73   72   71   70

1681694

Nicholas was a young pirate. But he was not like the rest of the pirates on the ship. They were rough and tough. Nicholas was a gentle pirate. In fact, sailing made him seasick.

Nicholas liked to spend his time feeding the fish that swam around the ship....

and growing flowers in the crow's-nest.

And he liked to invent things. He tied a barrel to the mast and made a shower bath.

He fastened a brush to a sailor's wooden leg to make scrubbing the deck easier.

And he attached a wheel to the captain's wooden leg.

Now the captain could spin all over the deck.

When the other pirates weren't busy with piracy, they drank rum and sang songs of the sea. But not Nicholas. He collected the empty bottles and built tiny ships inside them. And he dreamed of the day when he would leave the sea and make an honest living selling his ships in bottles.

Whenever the pirates came to land, Nicholas tried to run away. But the other pirates always caught him. Nicholas was so clever that they did not want to lose him.

It was Nicholas who always found the treasure other people buried on desert islands. For to tell the truth, these pirates were not very brave. They would rather steal treasure than fight for it.

Once, when they were being chased by a fleet of ships, the other pirates shook with fear. But Nicholas saved the day by painting the ship blue so it could not be seen against the ocean.

Nicholas's best friend was a pirate who had grown too old to be a sailor and now spent his days painting pictures. But one day the captain told him he was not earning his keep and would have to leave the ship.

As a parting gift, the old pirate told Nicholas a secret.
He knew the whereabouts of hidden treasure, and

he painted the treasure map on Nicholas's back.
But they did not notice that they were being spied on.

Nicholas thanked his friend and waved good-by.

Of course, the spy told Nicholas's secret, and the pirates chased him all over the ship. The captain got going so fast on his wheel that he couldn't stop, and he plunged into the sea.

Nicholas dove in to rescue him.

When the two were finally hoisted on deck, the pirates

found that the map had washed off Nicholas's back.
It was lost forever, and the treasure too.

In return for saving his life, the captain gave Nicholas
permission to leave the ship.

Nicholas was happy to be free. But he was all alone in the middle of the ocean. Not knowing where else to go, he set his course for the island the old pirate had told him about.

It was very hot on the desert island, so he took off his jacket. Suddenly he saw that the lining was covered with strange markings. It was the treasure map! While the paint on his back was still wet, the map had come off perfectly on his jacket.

Nicholas set right to work. He made several mistakes, because the map was now printed backward. But at last he uncovered an old leather chest full of gold.

1681694

Nicholas was rich. Now he would not have to earn his living selling ships in bottles. Then he stopped to think. How would he spend his time if he did not do what he liked best?

Nicholas found the answer. He ordered a huge
bottle made, and inside of it he built a great ship,

the biggest and finest one you can imagine.

And when it was finished, people came from everywhere
to see the biggest ship in a bottle in all the world.

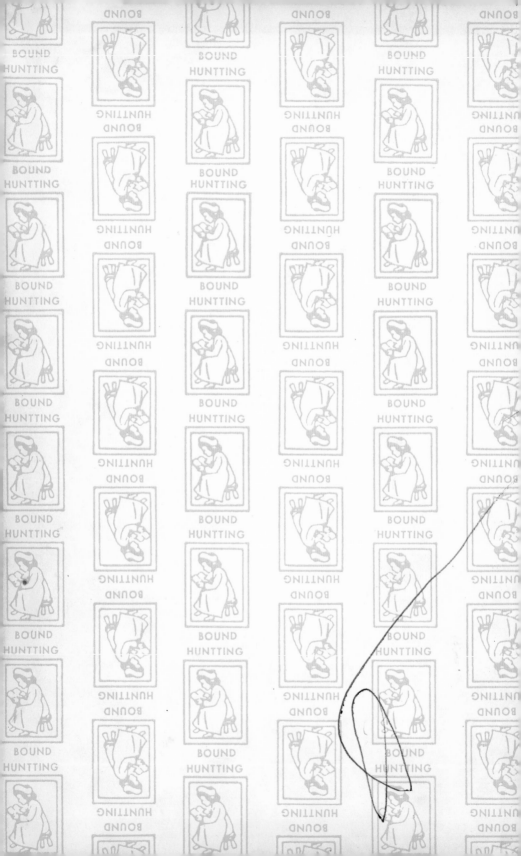